This book is to be returned on
the last date stamped below

The Little Tin Soldier

A PARRAGON BOOK

Published by
Parragon Books,
Unit 13-17, Avonbridge Trading Estate,
Atlantic Road, Avonmouth, Bristol BS11 9QD

Produced by
The Templar Company plc,
Pippbrook Mill, London Road, Dorking, Surrey RH4 1JE

Designed by Mark Kingsley-Monks

Printed and bound in Italy

ISBN 0-75250-919-5

The Little Tin Soldier

Retold by Stephanie Laslett
Illustrated by Helen Smith

That night, when everyone in the house was fast asleep, all the toys came out to play. They danced and jumped and laughed and sang and had a lovely time. But two toys did not join in the fun. They were the Tin Soldier and the Dancer and they stood perfectly still, looking straight at one another, for hour after hour.

When the Tin Soldier was taken from his box the first thing he saw was a pretty paper Dancer standing on one toe. She held her arms high above her head and the Tin Soldier thought she was the most beautiful lady he had ever seen!

"How I wish I could make her my wife," he sighed, "but she is too grand for me."

Once upon a time a small boy had a birthday. When he opened his present what should he find but twenty-five tin soldiers, packed side by side in a large wooden box. They were each exactly the same in every way, apart from just one. This soldier had been made last of all and the tin had run out just as it was being poured into his mould. When he was taken out to be painted it was discovered that he had just one leg, but he stood just as firm and steadfast on his one leg as the others did on two.

This was the brave Tin Soldier who had a great adventure and became famous, as you will soon see.

Suddenly the grandfather clock struck midnight and out from a snuff box jumped a little black imp.

"Hello, Tin Soldier!" he cried. "Why do you spend all your time looking at the Dancer? Don't you know that it's considered very rude to stare?"

But the Tin Soldier did not reply. He acted as if he had heard nothing at all.

"What impertinence!" snapped the imp. "I shall teach you a lesson. You just wait until tomorrow!" and with that he stamped his small foot and jumped back into the snuff box.

The next morning the little boy played happily with his tin soldiers and when his mother called him to lunch he placed the one-legged Tin Soldier upon the windowsill so that he could look out of the window.

Now whether it was the wind or whether it was the little black imp up to his tricks, who can tell, but all of a sudden the window flew up, the curtains flapped and out fell the little Tin Soldier.

Down he tumbled, head over heels, until he finally landed upside-down, bump! with his gun wedged firmly in between two paving stones.

As soon as the little boy returned from his meal he saw the open window and guessed what had happened. Out into the street he ran and there he searched high and low for his Tin Soldier.

The boy came so close to him that he almost trod on him and if the Soldier had only called out, "Here I am!" then he would surely have been found. But he was proud and believed that a Soldier should be able to look after himself and so he did not budge an inch or make so much as a whisper.

And so the Tin Soldier remained stuck between the stones, lost forever.

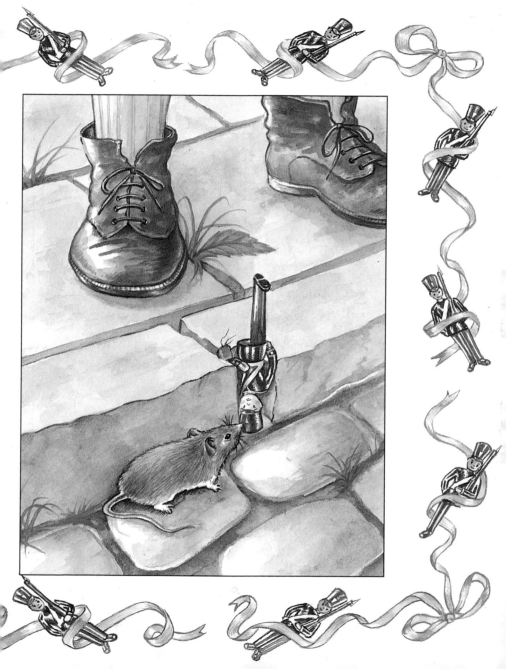

Soon the sky grew grey and it began to drizzle. The raindrops fell faster and faster and soon there was a steady downpour. But the Tin Soldier did not flinch. He held his gun straight and bore it all bravely.

When the rain finally stopped, two little street urchins came trotting along, busy looking for pennies on the wet pavement. Their eager eyes fell on the poor Tin Soldier and with shouts of glee they pulled him from his hole.

"Let us make a boat for him and then he can sail up and down like a regular Sea Admiral!" they cried.

In next to no time the Tin Soldier was standing upright in a paper boat and sailing down the gutter, whilst the boys ran beside him laughing delightedly. But soon the little stream flowed faster and faster. It was entering a tunnel!

The boys' excited shouts faded away behind him with the light and soon it was quite dark. The little Soldier trembled with fear but he gripped his gun tightly and stared straight ahead into the gloom. The water became rougher and large waves threatened to overturn him at any time.

Suddenly a great water rat poked his head out of the stream alongside the paper boat and glared angrily at the Tin Soldier.

"Show me your passport at once," he ordered. "Hurry up. You cannot travel down this tunnel without a passport!"

But the Tin Soldier never flinched. Silently he stared ahead and grasped his gun firmly to his shoulder.

"Stop him!" shouted the rat to the scraps of rubbish floating along the stream. "Stop that Tin Soldier immediately! He has not shown me his passport!" But the paper boat sped on down the dark tunnel and was soon beyond his reach.

The current in the water became swifter and stronger and soon the Tin Soldier was greatly relieved to see a glimpse of daylight ahead of him. The tunnel was ending at last. But what was that terrible roaring noise?

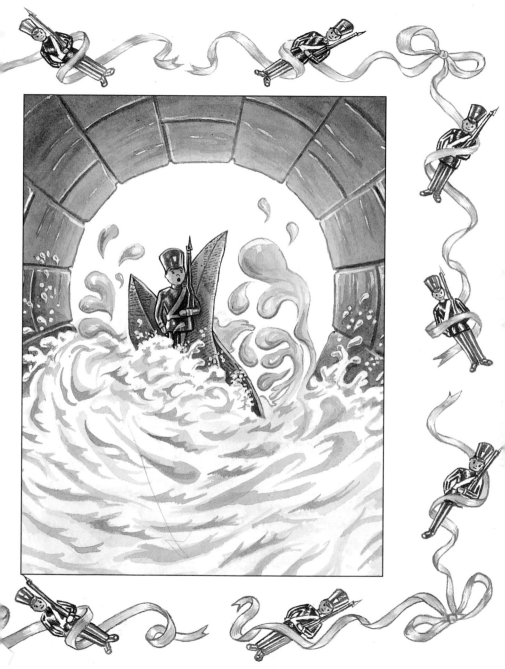

What a calamity! This was where the gutter emptied into a deep canal and at the mouth of the tunnel, the water rushed downwards in a great waterfall. Over the top went the little boat and the Tin Soldier knew he could not last much longer. The water hissed and boiled around him and at last he began to sink.

As he disappeared beneath the waves, the Tin Soldier stood straight to attention as best he could, for he wanted to be sure that no-one could ever after say that he had been a coward. So he slipped through the water — and at that very moment was swallowed up by a fish!

Oh, how dark it was inside the fish!
And how tightly squashed he felt!
"What has happened to me now?" the
Soldier wondered as he lay there, bravely
shouldering his gun, as upright as ever.

Up and down swam the fish, then all at once began to twist and thrash about. But just as soon as he had begun, the fish stopped moving and became still.

The Soldier lay quiet for a long time, not knowing where he was or what was to become of him. Then, in a flash, bright sunlight streamed over him. He found himself lying on a chopping board in a busy kitchen, next to a fine fish! The fish had been caught, taken to market, sold and now lay ready to be cooked!

"Well, just look who we have here!" exclaimed the cook, and she carried him upstairs and stood him on a table. And where was he? Why, back in his old home alongside his own tin brothers!

And there was the pretty Dancer, still patiently waiting with her arms held gracefully above her head. The Tin Soldier looked at her, unblinking, and she looked straight back at him.

All at once the little boy picked up the Tin Soldier and threw him straight in the fire! Why did he do such a thing? Who can say, but perhaps the little black imp might have had something to do with it.

The Soldier stood in the heart of the fire and although the heat must have been terrible, not once did he waver. He held his gun straight and gazed at the Dancer. The Dancer balanced on one toe and never took her eyes off the face of the brave Tin Soldier. A tear trickled down his cheek but whether it was the melting tin or whether it was the pain in his heart, who can tell?

Suddenly the door opened and a draught of air blew the little paper lady off the table. She flew through the air just like thistledown, then floated down towards the fire.

There stood the Tin Soldier as the flames licked around him. The Dancer flew straight into his arms and as her lips brushed his cheek she burst into flames.

Then the Tin Soldier finally softened and began to melt in the heat. His paint peeled away and at long last his gun fell from his shoulder and he began to buckle at the knees.

Next morning when the maid came to clear away the ashes, she found a tiny black cinder, all that was left of the little Dancer, and a small lump of tin in the shape of a heart - and that was all that remained of the brave Tin Soldier.

HANS CHRISTIAN ANDERSEN

Hans Andersen was born in Odense,
Denmark on April 2nd, 1805. His family
was very poor and throughout his life he
suffered much unhappiness. Even after he had
found success as a writer, Hans Andersen
felt something of an outsider;
an attitude which often emerged in his
stories, such as here in *The Steadfast Tin
Soldier*, published in 1838.
His fairy stories, famous throughout the
world, include *The Snow Queen*, *The Little
Mermaid* and *The Emperor's New Clothes*,
and are amongst the most frequently
translated works of literature.
He died in 1875.